LAUGHING
WITH
ANIMALS

A Joke Book for All Ages

Nadine Samardzija

ISBN: 9798746039941

Acknowledgements

Thank you to everyone who works to improve the lives of animals, including those who rescue and rehabilitate animals and those who focus on conservation efforts.

Thank you to the talented photographers. This book would not be what it is without your photographs.

Pixabay:
Alpaca: Manfred Richter
Baboon: Matan Nachmani
Bear: Marcel Langthim
Bird: Publix Domain Pictures
Chimpanzee: Republica
Crocodile: Myo Min Kway
Dolphin: n9akovic
Duck: Olga Okinskaya
Elephant: Neil Morrell
Flamingo: Heike Hartmann
Gorilla, Sheep, and Tiger: Alexas Fotos
Hippo and Wolf: Christel Sagniez
Horse: Liselotte Brunner
Lion: David Mark
Monkey: Lena Helfinger
Moose: Tommy Takacs
Orangutan: Herbert Aust
Orca: Jacqueline Schmid
Otter: Erik Stens
Panda: mordilla-net
Parrot: Susan Aken
Polar Bear: Onkel Ramirez
Reindeer: Steve Mantell
Turtle: Joe Velasquez

Other:
Cheetah, Penguin, Seal (cover), Zebra: Kevin Bedford, Natures Moments:
http://www.naturesmoments.co.uk/
Contact: email:
info@naturesmoments.co.uk

Cat: Christy Guggino, edited by Michael Kalinich

Giraffe and dogs: Nadine Samardzija

Shutterstock:
Cow: Oligo
Frog: Kurit Afshen
Kangaroo: Kent Townsend
Walrus: Aleksei Verhovski
Rabbit: Eric Isselee
Background on cover: 777_Designe

Freerange stock:
Pig: s86b

Table of Contents

Aardvark

What did the aardvark name its dog?

Aard-bark.

Alligator

What do you call an alligator in a vest?

An investigator.

What do you call an alligator that sneaks up behind you?

A tailgater.

What happens when an alligator drives a boat?

He becomes a navigator.

What do you call an alligator who stirs up trouble?

An instigator.

Alpaca

What do you call alpacas taking over the world?

The alpacalypse.

What do you call it when alpacas sing?

Alpacapella.

Angelfish
What do you call a fish in heaven?
Angelfish.

What do angelfish say to each other when they meet?
Halo.

Ant
What medicine would you give an ill ant?
Ant-ibiotics.

What do you call a well-dressed ant?
Elegant.

What kind of ant is good at math?
An accountant.

What do you call a 100-year-old ant?
An antique.

Anteater
Why don't anteaters get sick?
Because they are full of antibodies.

What do anteaters like on their pizza?
Ant-chovies.

Armadillo
What do you call a large group of armadillos?
Army-dillo.

Baboon
What do you call a
flying primate?
A hot air baboon.

What is a baboon's
favorite toy?
A ba-boom-orang.

Bat
What is the first thing bats learn in school?
The alpha-bat.

What exercise do bats do at night?
Aerobatics.

Bear
What do you call a wet bear?
A drizzly bear.

What do you call a bear with no teeth?
A gummy bear.

What did the teddy bear say after dinner?

I'm stuffed.

How can a bear catch fish without a pole?

They use their bear hands.

Why don't bears wear socks?

They like to go bear foot.

Bee

What did the bee say to the flower?

Hey bud.

What is the smartest insect?

A spelling bee.

I went to the beekeepers to buy some bees. Why didn't one of the bees have a price tag?

It was a freebee.

What do you call a bee who is having a bad hair day?

A frizz-bee.

What do you call a bee trying to make up its mind?

A maybe.

What kind of bee is bad at football?
A fumblebee.

Beetle

What do you call a nervous beetle?
A jitter-bug.

Why did the beetle get kicked out of the park?
Because he was a litter-bug.

Beluga

Why did the beluga go to the doctor?
It did not feel too whale.

Bird

What do you give a sick bird?
Tweetment.

What kind of bird works
at a construction site?
The crane.

Why do seagulls like to live
by the sea?

Because if they lived by the bay they would be called
baygulls.

Buffalo

What did the buffalo say to his son when he left for college?

Bison.

What's a buffalo's 200th birthday called?

A bisontennial.

Butterfly

What insect is the ruler of the insect world?

The monarch.

Camel

What did the camel say to the oasis?

I will never desert you.

What is a baby camel's favorite nursery rhyme?

Humpty Dumpty.

Cat

Why was the cat afraid of the tree?

Because of its bark.

What is a cat's favorite breakfast?

Mice krispies.

What kind of cats like to go bowling?

Alley cats.

What color do cats love the most?

Purrple.

What is a cat's favorite sticker?

Scratch and sniff.

Chameleon

What did the mom chameleon say to her nervous kid the first day of school?

Don't worry, you'll blend right in.

Cheetah

What is a cheetah's favorite food?

Fast food.

Why shouldn't you play cards in the savanna?

There are too many cheetahs.

What do you call a cheetah who uses a copy machine?

A copycat.

Chicken

What is the most musical part of a chicken?

The drumstick.

What do you call a funny chicken?

A comedi-hen.

What do chickens' study in college?

Egg-onomics.

Why didn't Mozart like chickens?

Because all they say is "Bach, Bach, Bach."

Why was the chicken kicked out of the baseball game?

They expected fowl play.

Chimpanzee

What is a chimpanzee's favorite cookie?

Chocolate Chimp.

What is a chimpanzee's favorite Christmas carol?

Jungle Bells.

What is a chimp's favorite month?

Ape-ril.

What do you call a chimp that wins at every sport?

Chimpion.

How do chimps get down the stairs?

They slide down the banana-ster.

Clownfish

What did one shark say to the other while eating a clownfish?

This tastes funny.

Cow

What do you call a cow that eats your grass?

A lawn moo-er.

Where do cows go on a Saturday night?

To the moooooovies.

Why do cows go to New York?

To see the moosicals.

What did the mama cow say to the baby cow?

It is pasture bedtime.

Crab

Why do crabs never share?

Because they are shellfish.

How did the crab hurt himself at the gym?

He pulled a mussel.

Where do crabs save their money?

In a sea bank.

How do crabs stay healthy?

Vitamin Sea.

Crocodile

What do you get when you cross a crocodile with a chicken?

A croc-a-doodle-doo.

Why can't crocodiles ever admit they're wrong?

Because they live in da Nile.

Deer

How do you compliment a deer?

Fawn over it.

What deer costs a dollar?

A buck.

What do you get when you cross a deer and a ghost?

Cariboo.

Dog

What happens when it rains cats and dogs?

You can step in a poodle.

What type of markets do dogs avoid?

Flea markets.

Did you hear the story about the golden retriever who brought a ball back from miles away?

It was far-fetched.

What did the hungry dalmatian say after he ate?

That hit the spot.

17

What do dogs like on their pizza?

Pupperoni.

What did the dog do after he ate a firefly?

He smiled with de-light.

What is a dog's favorite city?

New Yorkie.

What did the skeleton say to the puppy?

Bone Appetit.

What do you call a dog magician?

A labracadabrador.

Dolphin

What did the dolphin say to the blue whale?

Cheer up.

Why was the dolphin grumpy?

He ate too many crabs.

What did people say when the dolphin walked on water?

It was just a fluke.

Where do dolphins go to sleep?

In water beds.

Why do dolphins fail their school tests?

Because they work below the C level.

What is a dolphin's favorite holiday?

Findependence Day.

What did the magician say to the dolphin?

Pick a cod, any cod.

Donkey

What is a donkey's favorite game?

Pin the tail on the human.

What does a donkey do when you tell her a joke?

He-ha.

Duck

What do ducks watch on TV?

Duck-umentaries.

Why do ducks make good detectives?

They always quack the case.

What do ducks eat with soup?

Quackers.

What did the duck tell the waitress?

Put it on my bill.

What is a duck's favorite game?

Beak-a-boo.

What did the duck say to the comedian?

You quack me up.

When do ducks wake up?

At the quack of dawn.

Eagle

Why don't bald eagles tell knock knock jokes?

Because freedom rings.

Why shouldn't you hunt bald eagles?

It is ill-eagle.

Elephant

Where does an elephant pack his luggage?

In his trunk.

Why don't elephants use computers?

Because they are afraid of the mouse.

What do elephants and trees have in common?
They both have big trunks.

What do you call an unimportant elephant joke?
Irrelephant.

Firefly

How do fireflies start a race?
Ready, set, glow.

Fish

What is the difference between a fish and a piano?
You can't tuna fish.

What fish only swims at night?
A starfish.

Why are fish so smart?
Because they live in schools.

Why is it so easy to weigh fish?
Because they have their own scales.

What fish is most valuable?
The goldfish.

Flamingo
What is a flamingo's favorite game?
Fla-bingo.

Why did the flamingo go to
the salad bar?

For the shrimp.

Why did the flamingo
need a band aid?

It hurt its pinky.

How do flamingos search the internet?
With their webbed feet.

How do flamingos find friends?

They fla-mingle.

Frog

What happened when the frog's car broke down on the side of the road?

It got toad away.

What does a frog eat with his hamburger?

French flies.

Why are frogs so happy?

Because they eat whatever bugs them.

Why are frogs so good at basketball?

Because they always make jump shots.

What is a frog's favorite outfit?

A jumpsuit.

Gibbon

Why do gibbons like to make compromises?

They believe in gibbon take.

What happened when the gibbon failed his test?

He was gibbon another chance.

Giraffe

Why are giraffes slow to apologize?

Because it takes them a long time to swallow their pride.

Why are giraffes at the top of their class?

Because they are head and shoulders above everyone else.

Did you hear about the race between the ostrich and giraffe?

It was neck and neck.

Why wasn't the giraffe paying attention?

She had her head in the clouds.

Why do giraffes make bad pets?

They are high maintenance.

What did the dog say to the giraffe?

I have always looked up to you.

Goat

What do you call a goat that paints pictures?
Vincent Van Goat.

What do you call a goat with a beard?
Goatee.

Gorilla

Why did the gorilla fail its exam?
He did not have the ape-titude.

What is the first thing gorillas learn in school?
The ape b c's.

What do gorillas do when they get mad?
They go bananas.

What does a gorilla attorney study?
The law of the jungle.

Hippopotamus

What is a hippo's favorite music?
Hip-hop.

What do you call a hippo who does the opposite of what he says you should do?

Hippocrite.

What happens to hippos when they get too cold?

Hippothermia.

How do you get a hippo to do whatever you want?

Hippnotism.

What do you call a hippo who thinks he is sick?

Hippchondriac.

Horse

What sport do horses play?

Stable tennis.

Why did the foal go to the doctor?

He was a little horse.

What do you call a horse that likes to stay up late?

A night mare.

What makes a horse sneeze?

Hay fever.

What do you call a horse that lives next to you?

A neigh-bor.

Hyena

Did you hear about the hyena who drank a bowl of gravy?

He was the laughing stock.

Impala

What type of food do lions call impalas?

Fast food.

Jellyfish

What kind of fish goes well with peanut butter?

The jellyfish.

What makes a jelly fish laugh?

Ten tickles.

Kangaroo

What do you call a lazy baby kangaroo?

A pouch potato.

What did the kangaroo win a gold medal in?
In the long jump.

What is a kangaroo's favorite game?

Hopscotch.

What do you call two kangaroos who live together?

Roo-mates.

What is a kangaroo's favorite season?

Spring.

Koala

Why did the manager hire a koala?
Because he was koala-fied.

What type of research do koala's do?
Koalatative research.

Why did the koala quit his second job?
He needed koala-ty time with his family.

Lion

What do you call a lion wearing a stylish hat?

A dandy lion.

How does a lion move a canoe?

He uses his roar.

What state do lions like the most?

Maine.

What street do lions live on?

Mane Street.

What is a lion's favorite type of dance?

Lion dancing.

How do lions pass time?

By lion around.

Leopard

Why couldn't the leopard play hide and seek?

Because he was always spotted.

Manatee

What do manatees like to drink?

Mana-tea.

What is a manatee's favorite color?

Mana-teal.

Meerkat

Did you hear about the kitten who lived with a meerkat clan?

They did not realize she was a mere kat.

Monkey

What kind of key opens a banana?

A monkey.

What nickname do you give a monkey selling potato chips?

A chipmunk.

Why do monkeys love bananas?

Because they have appeal.

What part of the playground do monkeys love most?

The monkey bars.

What did the banana do when it saw a monkey?

The banana split.

What is a monkey's favorite tool?

A monkey wrench.

Moose

What do you call a moose that makes movies?
Deerector.

What do moose play at sleepovers?

Truth or deer.

What do you call a moose who is a celebrity?

Famoose.

Why do moose like comedians?
Because they are a-moose-ing.

What do you call a moose that plays piano?
A moosician.

What happened when the moose went rock climbing?
She held on for deer life.

Mouse

Why was the mouse afraid of the water?
Because of catfish.

What kind of cheese do mice like?
Mouserella.

How do you get a mouse to smile?
Say cheese.

What is a mouse's favorite game?
Hide and squeak.

What did the mouse say when he saw a cat?
You have got to be kitten me.

Octopus

What is an octopus's favorite shape?
An octagon.

Why was the octopus dangerous?
He was well armed.

Where does an octopus sleep when he is camping?
A tent-acle.

What do octopus knights wear?
A coat of arms.

What is an octopus's favorite month?

October.

Why can't an octopus commit a crime?

They do not have a bad bone in their body.

Opossum

What do you call a group of opossums?

A posse.

What kind of opossum goes back for more soup?

A more-supial.

Orangutan

What do you call an ape who works at a call center?

A who-rang-utang.

What do orangutans call their spouses?

Their prime-mate.

What is an ape's favorite fruit?

Ape-ricots.

What do you call an orangutan who likes lemon pies?
Meringue-utan

What do orangutans wear in the kitchen?
Ape-rons.

Orca Whale
Where do orca's hear music?
Orca-stras.

Why do orcas always get A's in school?

They do a killer job studying.

Where do orcas go to get braces?
Orca-dontist.

Why are orcas so good at hunting?
They are very well orca-strated.

Ostrich
What do you call an ostrich that practices dark magic?
An ostwitch.

What happened to the ostrich who could not fit in?
He was ostrich-sized.

Otter

Why did the otter become an astronaut?

He wanted to go to otter space.

What do you call an otter
who just got glasses?

A see otter.

Where do otters keep
their money?

In a riverbank.

What do otters drive?

An otter-mobile.

What should you do when you meet a famous otter?

Get their ottergraph.

Owl

Why do owls get invited to parties?

Because they are a hoot.

Panda

Why do pandas like old movies?

Because they are in black and white.

Why did the panda quit his job at the childcare center?

It was panda-monium.

What are pandas favorite breakfast food?

Panda-cakes.

How did the panda lose his meal?

It was bamboozled.

What happened to the pandas who got in a food fight?

They got bambooboos.

Parrot

What do you call a parrot after a bath?

Polly saturated.

What did the macaw say when he saw a duck?

Polly wants a quacker.

What is a parrot's favorite game?

Hide and speak.

What did the mom parrot say to her baby?
Beak-careful.

Where do the smartest parrots live?
In brain forests.

What did the parrot say on the 4th of July?
Polly wants a firecracker.

Why are parrots good at improvisation?
Because they know how to wing it.

Penguin
Why do penguins and polar bears not get along?
Because they are polar opposites.

Where do penguins
keep their money?

In a snowbank.

Why do penguins
wear glasses?
To help their ice-sight.

What did the sea say to the penguin?
Nothing, it just waved.

What is a penguin's favorite relative?

Aunt Arctica.

Pig

Why did the farmer call his pig "ink"?

Because it was always running out of the pen.

What did the pig say when he was out in the sun?

I'm bacon.

Why are pigs bad drivers?

They are road hogs.

What do you call an angry pig?

Disgruntled.

What do you call a pig who knows karate?

A pork chop.

What do pigs put on cuts?

Oinkment.

Polar bear

Where does a polar bear go to vote?

The north pole.

What dance do teenage polar bears go to?
The snow-ball.

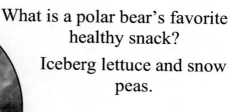

What is a polar bear's favorite healthy snack?

Iceberg lettuce and snow peas.

What is a polar bear's favorite shape?

Ice-oscleses triangle.

Porcupine

What do you get when you cross a porcupine and a turtle?
A slow poke.

What do you get when you cross a pig and a cactus?
A porky-pine.

Porpoise

What do porpoises clean with?
All-porpoise cleaner.

What did the porpoise say when he broke a toy?
I did not do it on porpoise.

Rabbit

Where do rabbits go after their wedding?

On a bunnymoon.

What do you call a group of rabbits hopping backwards?

A receding hare line.

What is a rabbit's favorite type of gold?

14 carrot gold.

What do you call a rabbit who is hopeful about the future?

A hop-timist.

What do you call a rich rabbit?

A millionhare.

Rat

What kind of car insurance do rats have?

Road dent insurance.

What do you call a rat who only likes to eat dessert?

A pie-rat.

How do you get a rat to smile?

Tell it cheesy jokes.

Why aren't rodents' good criminals?

Because someone always rats them out.

What do rats like to eat for dessert?

Mice cream.

Reindeer

What kind of deer is a good weather forecaster?

A rain-deer.

Did Rudolph go to school?

No, he was elf-taught.

Rhinoceros

How do rhinos like their eggs?

Anything but poached.

How do you stop a rhino from charging?

Take away its credit card.

Seal

What animals are on legal documents?

Seals.

Why did the seals shake hands?

To seal the deal.

What happened to the seal who encountered a polar bear?

His fate was sealed.

Sea Lion

What did the sea lion study in school?

Art Art Art Art.

Shark

Who is the builder of the sea?

A hammer head shark.

What happens when you cross a snowman and a shark?

Frostbite.

Where do sharks go on vacation?

Fin-land.

How did the hammerhead do on his test?

He nailed it.

Why did the shark cross the great barrier reef?

To get to the other tide.

Where do fish borrow money?
From a loan shark.

Sheep

Where did the sheep go on vacation?
The Baaaa-hamas.

What is a sheep's favorite food?
A candy baa.

What do you get if you cross a kangaroo with a sheep?
A woolly good jumper.

What swim stroke do sheep like the best?
Baaaackstroke.

What do sheep want to do?
To wool the world.

Skunk

Did you hear the latest joke about the skunk?
Never mind, it stunk.

How much money does a skunk have?
One scent.

What did the skunk say when he entered the courtroom?
Odor in the court.

What is a skunk's favorite school activity?
Show and smell.

What do you get when you cross a skunk with a chicken?
A fowl smell.

Snake
What is a snake's favorite subject?
Hiss-story.

What do you get when you cross a snake with a pie?
A pie-thon.

What is a snake's favorite dance?
The mamba.

Why was the snake mad at the jewel thief?
Because he wanted his diamond back.

Why are snakes hard to fool?
They have no legs to pull.

How do you make a baby snake cry?
Take away its rattle.

What do you call a funny snake joke?
Hissterical.

Spider
How do spiders communicate?
Through the World Wide Web.

What do you get when you cross spiders and corn?
Cobwebs.

What did the spider do when he became upset?
He went up the wall.

What occupation is the best fit for a spider?
A web designer.

Starfish
What do you call a famous fish?
A starfish.

Stingray
Why did the stingray talk to the scuba diver?
He wanted to have a manta man talk.

What is a stingray's favorite food?
Clam brulee

Tiger

Why didn't the boy
believe the tiger?

He thought it was
a lion.

What do you call
a tiger that likes
to dig in the sand?

Sandy Claws.

What is the difference between a cheetah and a lion?

A cheetah has the mane part missing.

Why do tigers have stripes?

So they don't get spotted.

Toad

What do you get if you cross a toad and a dog?

A croaker spaniel.

What is a toad's favorite game?

Croak-et.

Turtle

What kind of pictures do turtles take?

Shellfies.

What do you get when you cross a turtle with a giraffe?
A turtleneck.

How do turtles communicate?
With shellphones.

What did the cow say to the turtle?

Get a moooove on.

What kind of jokes do turtles tell?

Shell-arious ones.

What do you call a turtle that poops a lot?
Turdle.

Vulture
What do vultures do at parties?
They have scavenger hunts.

Why do vultures find it easy to fly?
They only have carrion luggage.

Walrus

What animal do you need
four of to build a house?

Wall-rus.

Why did the walrus
become a plumber?

Because he loves a tight seal.

What do you call a walrus special focus group?

A tusk force.

Whale

What is a whale's favorite sandwich?

Krilled Cheese.

What do you call a whale with bad posture?

A hunchback whale.

What do polite whales say?

You're whale-come.

What do whales like to chew?

Blubber gum.

What do whales like to paint with?

A-krill-ic paint.

Wolf

What do you call a woof that works as a lumber jack?

A timber wolf.

What do you call a wolf that meditates?

Aware-wolf.

What did one wolf say to the other?

Howl do you do?

What did the wolf say to the flea?

Stop bugging me.

What is a wolf's favorite fruit?

A pack of blueberries.

Yak

How does a yak win the lottery?

By hitting the yak-pot.

What do you call a yak that will not stop talking?

Yakkety Yak.

Zebra

What is a zebra's favorite food?

Grevy.

Why don't zebras like to color?

They do not like to stay between the lions.

What do you get when you cross a zebra with a fish?

Seabra.

Made in the USA
Middletown, DE
09 December 2021

54968755R00029